FLUTE PLAYALONG
Showtunes

WISE PUBLICATIONS
PART OF THE MUSIC SALES GROUP

LONDON / NEW YORK / PARIS / SYDNEY / COPENHAGEN / BERLIN / MADRID / HONG KONG / TOKYO

Published by

WISE PUBLICATIONS
14-15 Berners Street, London W1T 3LJ, UK

Exclusive Distributors:

MUSIC SALES LIMITED
Distribution Centre, Newmarket Road,
Bury St Edmunds, Suffolk IP33 3YB, UK

MUSIC SALES PTY LIMITED
20 Resolution Drive,
Caringbah, NSW 2229, Australia

Order No. AM1000329
ISBN 978-1-84938-505-3
This book © Copyright 2010 Wise Publications,
a division of Music Sales Limited.

Edited by Lizzie Moore.
CD recorded, mixed and mastered by Jonas Persson.
Engraved by Camden Music.
Cover designed & illustrated by Lizzie Barrand.

Printed in the EU

www.musicsales.com

YOUR GUARANTEE OF QUALITY
As publishers, we strive to produce every book
to the highest commercial standards.
The music has been freshly engraved and the book has
been carefully designed to minimise awkward page turns
and to make playing from it a real pleasure.
Particular care has been given to specifying acid-free,
neutral-sized paper made from pulps which have not been
elemental chlorine bleached. This pulp is from farmed
sustainable forests and was produced with special regard
for the environment.
Throughout, the printing and binding have been planned
to ensure a sturdy, attractive publication which should
give years of enjoyment.
If your copy fails to meet our high standards,
please inform us and we will gladly replace it.

Flute Fingering Chart

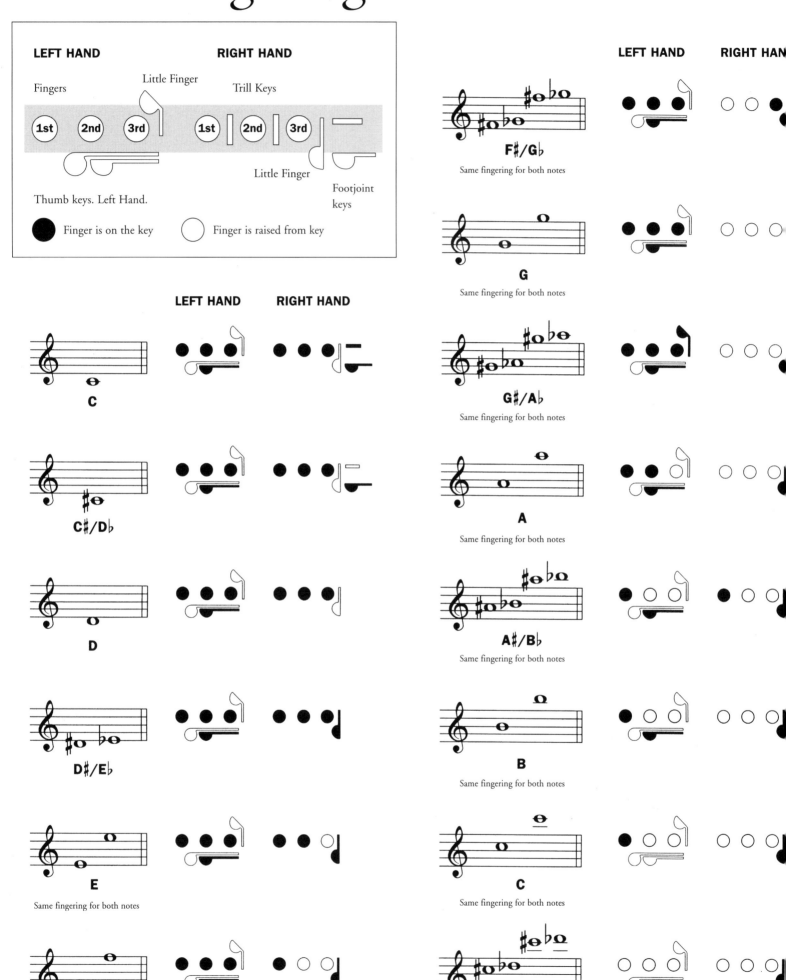

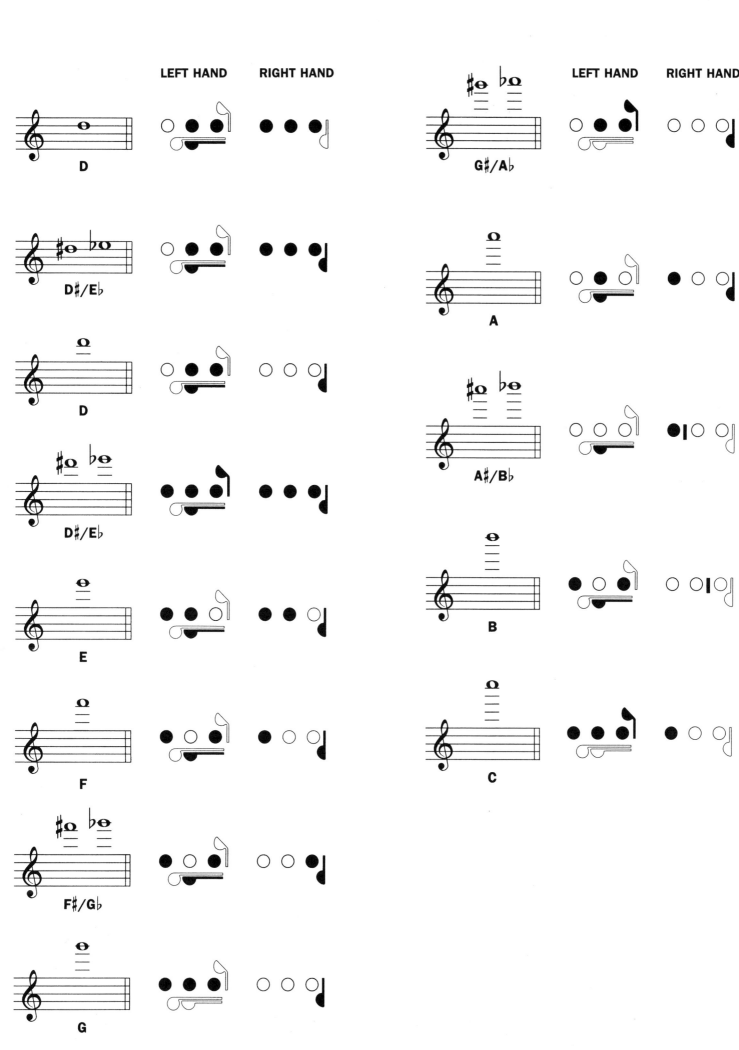

ANY DREAM WILL DO
(FROM 'JOSEPH AND THE AMAZING TECHNICOLOR® DREAMCOAT')

Words by Tim Rice
Music by Andrew Lloyd Webber

AS LONG AS HE NEEDS ME (FROM 'OLIVER!')

Words & Music by Lionel Bart

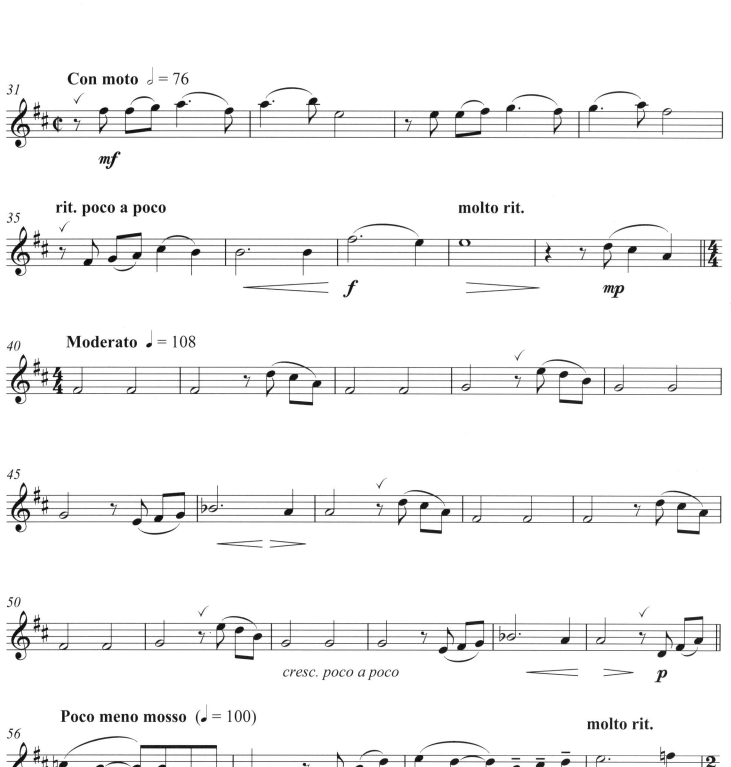

BIG SPENDER (FROM 'SWEET CHARITY')

Music by Cy Coleman

D.S. al Coda

𝄋 **Coda**

Breaking Free (FROM 'HIGH SCHOOL MUSICAL')

Words & Music by Jamie Houston

BRING HIM HOME (FROM 'LES MISÉRABLES')

Words by Alain Boublil & Herbert Kretzmer
Music by Claude-Michel Schönberg

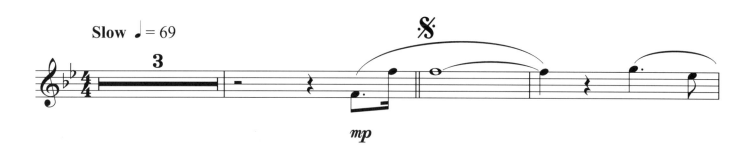

to Coda ⊕

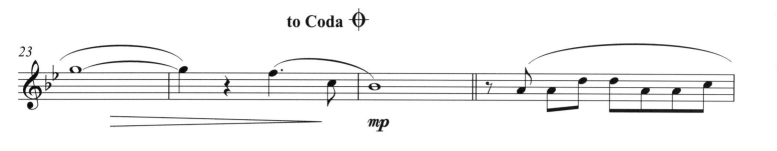

D.S. al Coda

⊕ **Coda**

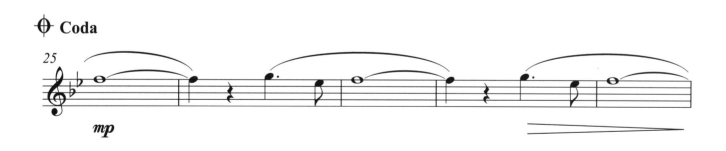

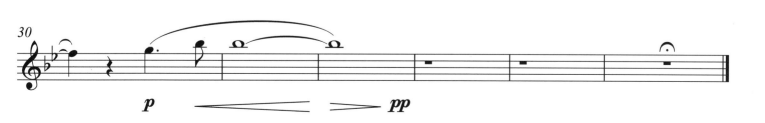

Can You Feel The Love Tonight
(from Walt Disney Pictures' 'The Lion King')

Words by Tim Rice
Music by Elton John

THE CANDY MAN
(FROM 'WILLY WONKA & THE CHOCOLATE FACTORY')

Words & Music by Leslie Bricusse & Anthony Newley

With a bright swing ♩ = 140

mf dolce

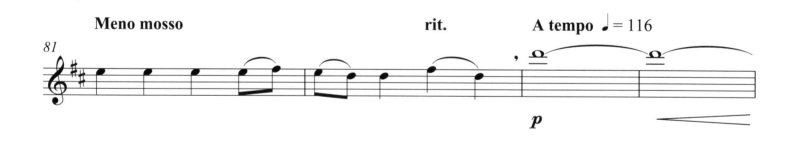

Don't Cry For Me Argentina (from 'Evita')

Words by Tim Rice
Music by Andrew Lloyd Webber

Slow tango feel

poco rall.   **Slower**

(Strings cue)

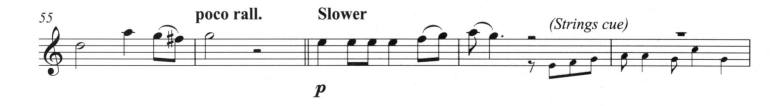

Tempo 1º

Slower and freely

rit.

Refrain grandioso

molto
allargando

a tempo

ELECTRICITY (FROM 'BILLY ELLIOT THE MUSICAL')

Words by Lee Hall
Music by Elton John

mp legato

mf

f

molto rit.   Broadly ♩ = 80

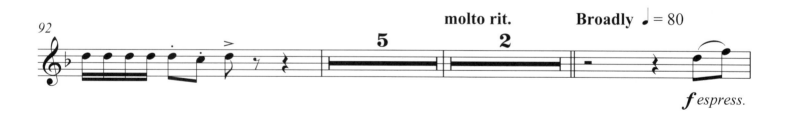

f espress.

molto rit.　　　a tempo

HOPELESSLY DEVOTED TO YOU (FROM 'GREASE')

Words & Music by John Farrar

Pseudo 50s rock 'n' roll ballad ♩. = 73

I Don't Know How To Love Him
(FROM 'JESUS CHRIST SUPERSTAR')

Words by Tim Rice
Music by Andrew Lloyd Webber

I DREAMED A DREAM (FROM 'LES MISÉRABLES')

Original Words by Alain Boublil & Jean-Marc Natel
English Words by Herbert Kretzmer
Music by Claude-Michel Schönberg

I Know Him So Well (From 'Chess')

Words by Tim Rice
Music by Benny Andersson & Björn Ulvaeus

If I Were A Rich Man

(from 'Fiddler On The Roof')

Words by Sheldon Harnick
Music by Jerry Bock

D.S. al Coda

Coda

Slower

Tempo 1º

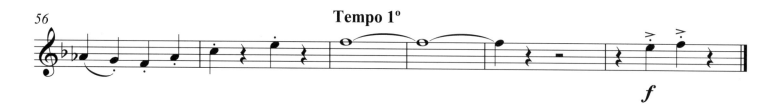

MY FAVORITE THINGS (FROM 'THE SOUND OF MUSIC')

Words by Oscar Hammerstein
Music by Richard Rodgers

Tunefully, in 1 ♩. = c.73

LOVE CHANGES EVERYTHING
(FROM 'ASPECTS OF LOVE')

Words by Don Black & Charles Hart
Music by Andrew Lloyd Webber

MEMORY (FROM 'CATS')

Words by Trevor Nunn after T.S. Eliot
Music by Andrew Lloyd Webber

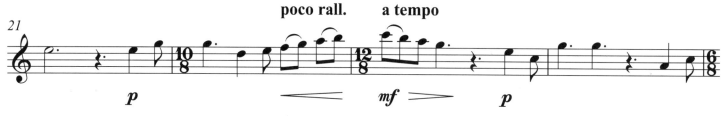

On My Own (FROM 'LES MISÉRABLES')

Original French Words by Alain Boublil & Jean-Marc Natel
English Words by Herbert Kretzmer, Trevor Nunn & John Caird
Music by Claude-Michel Schönberg

Sadly, espressivo e rubato ♩ = c.72

Cor Anglais

With a more definite pulse, gradually building

mp warmly

mf

Poco più mosso

f *appassionato*

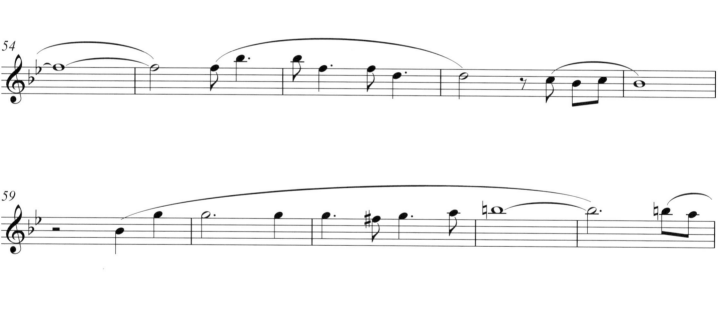

ff

ONE DAY I'LL FLY AWAY (FROM 'MOULIN ROUGE!')

Words by Will Jennings
Music by Joe Sample

SMOKE GETS IN YOUR EYES (FROM 'ROBERTA')

Words by Otto Harbach
Music by Jerome Kern

Ballad, classically ♩ = 72

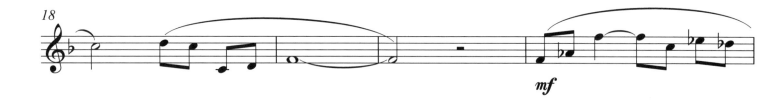

123456789

CD Track Listing

Disc 1

Full performance tracks...

1. Any Dream Will Do
(Webber/Rice) The Really Useful Group Limited.

2. As Long As He Needs Me
(Bart) Lakeview Music Publishing Company Limited.

3. Big Spender
(Coleman) Campbell Connelly & Co. Limited.

4. Breaking Free
(Houston) Warner/Chappell Artemis Music Limited.

5. Bring Him Home
(Schönberg/Boublil/Kretzmer) Alain Boublil Music Limited.

6. Can You Feel The Love Tonight
(Rice/John) Warner/Chappell Artemis Music Limited.

7. The Candy Man
(Bricusse/Newley) Universal Music Publishing Limited.

8. Don't Cry For Me Argentina
(Webber/Rice) Evita Music Limited.

9. Electricity
(Hall/John) Universal Music Publishing Limited.

10. Hopelessly Devoted To You
(Farrar) Sony/ATV Harmony (UK) Limited.

11. I Don't Know How To Love Him
(Webber/Rice) Universal/MCA Music Limited.

12. I Dreamed A Dream
(Schönberg/Boublil/Natel/Kretzmer) Alain Boublil Music Limited.

13. I Know Him So Well
(Rice/Andersson/Ulvaeus) Universal Music Publishing Limited.

14. If I Were A Rich Man
(Harnick/Bock) Carlin Music Corporation.

15. My Favorite Things
(Hammerstein/Rodgers) Imagem Music.

16. Love Changes Everything
(Webber/Black/Hart) The Really Useful Group Limited.

17. Memory
(Webber/Nunn/Eliot) The Really Useful Group Limited/Faber Music Limited.

18. On My Own
(Schönberg/Boublil/Natel/Kretzmer/Nunn/Caird) Alain Boublil Music Limited.

19. One Day I'll Fly Away
(Jennings/Sample) Universal Music Publishing Limited/Chrysalis Music Limited.

20. Smoke Gets In Your Eyes
(Harbach/Kern) Universal Music Publishing Limited.

Disc 2

Backing tracks only...

1. Any Dream Will Do

2. As Long As He Needs Me

3. Big Spender

4. Breaking Free

5. Bring Him Home

6. Can You Feel The Love Tonight

7. The Candy Man

8. Don't Cry For Me Argentina

9. Electricity

10. Hopelessly Devoted To You

11. I Don't Know How To Love Him

12. I Dreamed A Dream

13. I Know Him So Well

14. If I Were A Rich Man

15. My Favorite Things

16. Love Changes Everything

17. Memory

18. On My Own

19. One Day I'll Fly Away

20. Smoke Gets In Your Eyes